THE DEVIL IN IRON

BY

ROBERT E. HOWARD

British Library Cataloguing-in-Publication Data
A catalogue record for this book is available from the
British Library

Contents

Robert E. Howard. 1

I. 3

II. 8

III 15

IV 19

V. 31

VI 38

Robert E. Howard

Robert Ervin Howard was born in Peaster, Texas in 1906. During his youth, his family moved between a variety of Texan boomtowns, and Howard – a bookish and somewhat introverted child – was steeped in the violent myths and legends of the Old South. Although he loved reading and learning, Howard developed a distinctly Texan, hardboiled outlook on the world. He became a passionate fan of boxing, taking it up at an amateur level, and from the age of nine began to write adventure tales of semi-historical bloodshed. In 1919, when Howard was thirteen, his family moved to the Central Texas hamlet of Cross Plains, where he would stay for the rest of his life.

At fifteen Howard began to read the pulp magazines of the day, and to write more seriously. The December 1922 issue of his high school newspaper featured two of his stories, 'Golden Hope Christmas' and 'West is West'. In 1924 he sold his first piece – a short caveman tale titled 'Spear and Fang' – for $16 to the not-yet-famous *Weird Tales* magazine. He published with the magazine regularly over the next few years. 1929 was a breakout year for Howard, in that the 23-year-old writer began to sell to other magazines, such as *Ghost Stories* and *Argosy*, both of whom had previously sent him hundreds of rejection slips. In 1930, he began a correspondence with weird fiction master H. P. Lovecraft which ran up to his death six years later, and is regarded as one of the great correspondence cycles in all of fantasy literature.

It was partly due to Lovecraft's encouragement that Howard created his most famous character, Conan the Cimmerian. Conan – a barbarian-turned-King during the Hyborian Age, a mythical period of some 12,000 years ago – featured in seventeen *Weird Tales* stories between 1933 and 1936, and is now regarded as having spawned the 'sword and sorcery' genre, making Howard's influence on fantasy literature comparable to that of J. R. R. Tolkien's. The Conan stories have since been adapted many times, most famously in the series of films starring Arnold Schwarzenegger.

Howard was enjoying an all-time high in sales by the beginning of 1936, but he was also deeply upset by the ill health of his mother, who had fallen into a coma. On the morning of June 11, 1936, he asked an attending nurse whether she would ever recover, and the nurse replied negatively. Howard walked to his car, parked outside the family home in Cross Plains, and shot himself. He died eight hours later, aged just thirty.

I

The fisherman loosened his knife in its scabbard. The gesture was instinctive, for what he feared was nothing a knife could slay, not even the saw-edged crescent blade of the Yuetshi that could disembowel a man with an upward stroke. Neither man nor beast threatened him in the solitude which brooded over the castellated isle of Xapur.

He had climbed the cliffs, passed through the jungle that bordered them, and now stood surrounded by evidences of a vanished state. Broken columns glimmered among the trees, the straggling lines of crumbling walls meandered off into the shadows, and under his feet were broad paves, cracked and bowed by roots growing beneath.

The fisherman was typical of his race, that strange people whose origin is lost in the gray dawn of the past, and who have dwelt in their rude fishing huts along the southern shore of the Sea of Vilayet since time immemorial. He was broadly built, with long, apish arms and a mighty chest, but with lean loins and thin, bandy legs. His face was broad, his forehead low and retreating, his hair thick and tangled. A belt for a knife and a rag for a loin cloth were all he wore in the way of clothing.

That he was where he was proved that he was less dully incurious than most of his people. Men seldom visited

3

Xapur. It was uninhabited, all but forgotten, merely one among the myriad isles which dotted the great inland sea. Men called it Xapur, the Fortified, because of its ruins, remnants of some prehistoric kingdom, lost and forgotten before the conquering Hyborians had ridden southward. None knew who reared those stones, though dim legends lingered among the Yuetshi which half intelligibly suggested a connection of immeasurable antiquity between the fishers and the unknown island kingdom.

But it had been a thousand years since any Yuetshi had understood the import of these tales; they repeated them now as a meaningless formula, a gibberish framed to their lips by custom. No Yuetshi had come to Xapur for a century. The adjacent coast of the mainland was uninhabited, a reedy marsh given over to the grim beasts that haunted it. The fisher's village lay some distance to the south, on the mainland. A storm had blown his frail fishing craft far from his accustomed haunts and wrecked it in a night of flaring lightning and roaring waters on the towering cliffs of the isle. Now, in the dawn, the sky shone blue and clear; the rising sun made jewels of the dripping leaves. He had climbed the cliffs to which he had clung through the night because, in the midst of the storm, he had seen an appalling lance of lightning fork out of the black heavens, and the concussion of its stroke, which had shaken the whole island, had been accompanied by a cataclysmic crash that he doubted could have resulted from a riven tree.

A dull curiosity had caused him to investigate; and now he had found what he sought, and an animal-like uneasiness possessed him, a sense of lurking peril.

Among the trees reared a broken domelike structure, built of gigantic blocks of the peculiar ironlike green stone found only on the islands of Vilayet. It seemed incredible that human hands could have shaped and placed them, and certainly it was beyond human power to have overthrown the structure they formed. But the thunderbolt had splintered the ton-heavy blocks like so much glass, reduced others to green dust, and ripped away the whole arch of the dome.

The fisherman climbed over the debris and peered in, and what he saw brought a grunt from him. Within the ruined dome, surrounded by stone dust and bits of broken masonry, lay a man on a golden block. He was clad in a sort of skirt and a shagreen girdle. His black hair, which fell in a square mane to his massive shoulders, was confined about his temples by a narrow gold band. On his bare, muscular breast lay a curious dagger with a jeweled pommel, a shagreen-bound hilt, and a broad, crescent blade. It was much like the knife the fisherman wore at his hip, but it lacked the serrated edge and was made with infinitely greater skill.

The fisherman lusted for the weapon. The man, of course, was dead; had been dead for many centuries. This dome was his tomb. The fisherman did not wonder by what art the ancients had preserved the body in such a vivid likeness of life, which kept the muscular limbs full and unshrunken, the dark flesh vital. The dull brain of the Yuetshi had room only for his desire for the knife with its delicate, waving lines along the dully gleaming blade.

Scrambling down into the dome, he lifted the weapon from the man's breast. As he did so, a strange and terrible thing came to pass. The muscular, dark hands knotted convulsively, the lids flared open, revealing great, dark, magnetic eyes, whose stare struck the startled fisherman like a physical blow. He recoiled, dropping the jeweled dagger in his perturbation. The man on the dais heaved up to a sitting position, and the fisherman gaped at the full extent of his size, thus revealed. His narrowed eyes held the Yuetshi, and in those slitted orbs he read neither friendliness nor gratitude; he saw only a fire as alien and hostile as that which burns in the eyes of a tiger.

Suddenly the man rose and towered above him, menace in his every aspect. There was no room in the fisherman's dull brain for fear, at least for such fear as might grip a man who has just seen the fundamental laws of nature defied. As the great hands fell to his shoulders, he drew his saw-edged knife and struck upward with the same motion. The blade splintered against the stranger's corded belly as against a steel column, and then the fisherman's thick neck broke like a rotten twig in the giant hands.

II

Jehungir Agha, lord of Khawarizm and keeper of the costal border, scanned once more the ornate parchment scroll with its peacock seal and laughed shortly and sardonically.

"Well?" bluntly demanded his counsellor Ghaznavi.

Jehungir shrugged his shoulders. He was a handsome man, with the merciless pride of birth and accomplishment.

"The king grows short of patience," he said. "In his own hand he complains bitterly of what he calls my failure to guard the frontier. By Tarim, if i cannot deal a blow to these robbers of the steppes, Khawarizm may own a new lord."

Ghaznavi tugged his gray-shot beard in meditation. Yezdigerd, king of Turan, was the mightiest monarch in the world. In his palace in the great port city of Aghrapur was heaped the plunder of empires. His fleets of purple-sailed war galleys had made Vilayet an Hyrkanian lake. The dark-skinned people of Zamora paid him tribute, as did the eastern provinces of Koth. The Shemites bowed to his rule as far west as Shushan. His armies ravaged the borders of Stygia in the south and the snowy lands of the Hyperboreans in the north. His riders bore torch and sword westward into Brythunia and Ophir and Corinthia, even to the borders of Nemedia. His gilt-helmeted swordsmen had trampled hosts under their horses' hoofs, and walled cities went up in flames at his command. In the glutted slave markets of Aghrapur, Sultanapur, Khawarizm, Shahpur, and Khorusun, women were sold for three small silver coins — blonde Brythunians, tawny Stygians, dark-haired Zamorians, ebon Kushites, olive-skinned Shemites.

Yet, while his swift horsemen overthrew armies far from his frontiers, at his very borders an audacious foe plucked his beard with a red-dripping and smoke-stained hand.

On the broad steppes between the Sea of Vilayet and the borders of the easternmost Hyborian kingdoms, a new race had sprung up in the past half-century, formed originally of fleeing criminals, broken men, escaped slaves, and deserting soldiers. They were men of many crimes and countries, some born on the steppes, some fleeing from the kingdoms in the West. They were called kozak, which means wastrel.

Dwelling on the wild, open steppes, owning no law but their own peculiar code, they had become a people capable even of defying the Grand Monarch. Ceaselessly they raided the Turanian frontier, retiring in the steppes when defeated; with the pirates of Vilayet, men of much the same breed, they harried the coast, preying off the merchant ships which plied between the Hyrkanian ports.

"How am I to crush these wolves?" demanded Jehungir. "If I follow them into the steppes, I run the risk either of being cut off and destroyed, or of having them elude me

9

entirely and burn the city in my absence. Of late they have been more daring than ever."

"That is because of the new chief who has risen among them," answered Ghaznavi. "You know whom I mean."

"Aye!" replied Jehungir feelingly. "It is that devil Conan; he is even wilder than the kozaks, yet he is crafty as a mountain lion."

"It is more through wild animal instinct than through intelligence," answered Ghaznavi. "The other kozaks are at least descendants of civilized men. He is a barbarian. But to dispose of him would be to deal them a crippling blow."

"But how?" demanded Jehungir. "He has repeatedly cut his way out of spots that seemed certain death for him. And, instinct or cunning, he has avoided or escaped every trap set for him."

"For every beast and for every man there is a trap he will not escape," quoth Ghaznavi. "When we have parleyed with the kozaks for the ransom of captives, I have observed this man Conan. He has a keen relish for women and strong drink. Have your captive Octavia fetched here."

Jehungir clapped his hands, and an impressive Kushite eunuch, an image of shining ebony in silken pantaloons, bowed before him and went to do his bidding. Presently he returned, leading by the wrist a tall, handsome girl, whose yellow hair, clear eyes, and fair skin identified her as a pure-blooded member of her race. Her scanty silk tunic, girded at the waist, displayed the marvelous contours of her magnificent figure. Her fine eyes flashed with resentment and her red lips were sulky, but submission had been taught her during her captivity. She stood with hanging head before her master until he motioned her to a seat on the divan beside him. Then he looked inquiringly at Ghaznavi.

"We must lure Conan away from the kozaks," said the counsellor abruptly. "Their war camp is at present pitched somewhere on the lower reaches of the Zaporoska River — which, as you well know, is a wilderness of reeds, a swampy jungle in which our last expedition was cut to pieces by those masterless devils."

"I am not likely to forget that," said Jehungir wryly.

"There is an uninhabited island near the mainland," said Ghaznavi, "known as Xapur, the Fortified, because of some ancient ruins upon it. There is a peculiarity about it which makes it perfect for our purpose. It has no shoreline but rises sheer out of the sea in cliffs a hundred and fifty feet tall. Not even an ape could negotiate them. The only place where a man can go up or down is a narrow path on the western side that has the appearance of a worn stair, carved into the solid rock of the cliffs.

"If we could trap Conan on that island, alone, we could hunt him down at our leisure, with bows, as men hunt a lion."

"As well wish for the moon," said Jehungir impatiently. "Shall we send him a messenger, bidding him climb the cliffs and await our coming?"

"In effect, yes!" Seeing Jehungir's look of amazement, Ghaznavi continued: "We will ask for a parley with the kozaks in regard to prisoners, at the edge of the steppes by Fort Ghori. As usual, we will go with a force and encamp outside the castle. They will come, with an equal force, and the parley will go forward with the usual distrust and suspicion. But this time we will take with us, as if by casual chance, your beautiful captive." Octavia changed color and listened with intensified interest as the counsellor nodded toward her. "She will use all her wiles to attract Conan's attention. That should not be difficult. To that wild reaver, she should appear a dazzling vision of loveliness. Her vitality and substantial figure should appeal to him more vividly than would one of the doll-like beauties of your seraglio."

Octavia sprang up, her white fists clenched, her eyes blazing and her figure quivering with outraged anger.

"You would force me to play the trollop with this barbarian?" she exclaimed. "I will not! I am no market-block slut to smirk and ogle at a steppes robber. I am the daughter of a Nemedian lord—"

"You were of the Nemedian nobility before my riders carried you off," returned Jehungir cynically. "Now you are merely a slave who will do as she is bid."

"I will not!" she raged.

"On the contrary," rejoined Jehungir with studied cruelty, "you will. I like Ghaznavi's plan. Continue, prince among counsellors."

"Conan will probably wish to buy her. You will refuse to sell her, of course, or to exchange her for Hyrkanian prisoners. He may then try to steal her, or take her by force — though I do not think even he would break the parley truce. Anyway, we must be prepared for whatever he might attempt.

"Then, shortly after the parley, before he has time to forget all about her, we will send a messenger to him, under a flag of truce, accusing him of stealing the girl and demanding her return. He may kill the messenger, but at least he will think that she has escaped.

"Then we will send a spy — a Yuetishi fisherman will do — to the kozak camp, who will tell Conan that Octavia is hiding on Xapur. If I know my man, he will go straight to that place."

"But we do not know that he will go alone," Jehungir argued.

"Does a man take a band of warriors with him, when going to a rendezvous with a woman he desires?" retorted Ghaznavi. "The chances are all that he will go alone. But we will take care of the other alternative. We will not await him on the island, where we might be trapped ourselves, but among the reeds of a marshy point, which juts out to within a thousand yards of Xapur. If he brings a large force, we'll beat a retreat and think up another plot. If he comes alone or with a small party, we will have him. Depend upon it, he will come, remembering your charming slave's smiles and meaning glances."

"I will never descend to such shame!" Octavia was wild with fury and humiliation. "I will die first!"

"You will not die, my rebellious beauty," said Jehungir, "but you will be subjected to a very painful and humiliating experience."

He clapped his hands, and Octavia palled. This time it was not the Kushite who entered, but a Shemite, a heavily muscled man of medium height with a short, curled, blue-black beard.

"Here is work for you, Gilzan," said Jehungir. "Take this fool, and play with her awhile. Yet be careful not to spoil her beauty."

With an inarticulate grunt the Shemite seized Octavia's wrist, and at the grasp of his iron fingers, all the defiance went out of her. With a piteous cry she tore away and threw herself on her knees before her implacable master, sobbing incoherently for mercy.

Jehungir dismissed the disappointed torturer with a gesture, and said to Ghaznavi: "If your plan succeeds, I will fill your lap with gold."

III

In the darkness before dawn, an unaccustomed sound disturbed the solitude that slumbered over the reedy marshes and the misty waters of the coast. It was not a drowsy waterfowl nor a waking beast. It was a human who struggled through the thick reeds, which were taller than a man's head.

It was a woman, had there been anyone to see, tall, and yellow-haired, her splendid limbs molded by her draggled tunic. Octavia had escaped in good earnest, every outraged fiber of her still tingling from her experience in a captivity that had become unendurable.

Jehungir's mastery of her had been bad enough; but with deliberate fiendishness Jehungir had given her to a nobleman whose name was a byword for degeneracy even in Khawarizm.

Octavia's resilient flesh crawled and quivered at her memories. Desperation had nerved her climb from Jelal Khan's castle on a rope made of strips from torn tapestries, and chance had led her to a picketed horse. She had ridden all night, and dawn found her with a foundered steed on the swampy shores of the sea. Quivering with the abhorence of being dragged back to the revolting destiny planned for her by Jelal Khan, she plunged into the morass, seeking a hiding place from the pursuit she expected. When the reeds grew thinner around her and the water rose about her thighs, she saw the dim loom of an island ahead of her. A broad span of water lay between, but she did not hesitate. She waded out until the low waves were lapping about her waist; then she struck out strongly, swimming with a vigor that promised unusual endurance.

As she neared the island, she saw that it rose sheer from the water in castlelike cliffs. She reached them at last but found neither ledge to stand on below the water, nor to cling to above. She swam on, following the curve of the cliffs, the strain of her long flight beginning to weight her limbs. Her hands fluttered along the sheer stone, and suddenly they found a depression. With a sobbing gasp of relief, she pulled herself out of the water and clung there, a dripping white goddess in the dim starlight.

She had come upon what seemed to be steps carved in the cliff. Up them she went, flattening herself against the stone as she caught a faint clack of muffled oars. She strained her eyes and thought she made out a vague bulk moving toward the reedy point she had just quitted. But it was too far away for her to be sure in the darkness, and presently the faint sound ceased and she continued her climb. If it were her pursuers, she knew of no better course than to hide on the island. She knew that most of the islands off that marshy coast were uninhabited. This might be a pirate's lair, but even pirates would be preferable to the beast she had escaped.

A vagrant thought crossed her mind as she climbed, in which she mentally compared her former master with the kozak chief with whom — by compulsion — she had shamefully flirted in the pavillions of the camp by Fort Ghori, where the Hyrkanian lords had parleyed with the warriors of the steppes. His burning gaze had frightened and humiliated her, but his cleanly elemental fierceness set him above Jelal Khan, a monster such as only an overly opulent civilization can produce.

She scrambled up over the cliff edge and looked timidly at the dense shadows which confronted her. The trees grew close to the cliffs, presenting a solid mass of blackness. Something whirred above her head and she cowered, even though realizing it was only a bat.

She did not like the looks of those ebony shadows, but she set her teeth and went toward them, trying not to think of snakes. Her bare feet made no sound in the spongy loam under the trees.

Once among them, the darkness closed frighteningly about her. She had not taken a dozen steps when she was no longer able to look back and see the cliffs and the sea beyond. A few steps more and she became hopelessly confused and lost her sense of direction. Through the tangled branches not even a star peered. She groped and floundered on, blindly, and then came to a sudden halt.

Somewhere ahead there began the rhythmical booming of a drum. It was not such a sound as she would have expected to hear in that time and place. Then she forgot it as she was aware of a presence near her. She could not see, but she knew that something was standing beside her in the darkness.

With a stifled cry she shrank back, and as she did so, something that even in her panic she recognized as a human arm curved about her waist. She screamed and threw all her supple young strength into a wild lunge for freedom, but her captor caught her up like a child, crushing her frantic resistance with ease. The silence with which her frenzied pleas and protests were received added to her terror as she felt herself being carried through the darkness toward the distant drum, which still pulsed and muttered.

IV

As the first tinge of dawn reddened the sea, a small boat with a solitary occupant approached the cliffs. The man in the boat was a picturesque figure. A crimson scarf was knotted about his head; his wide silk breeches, of flaming hue, were upheld by a broad sash, which likewise supported a scimitar in a shagreen scabbard. His gilt-worked leather boots suggested the horseman rather than the seaman, but he handled his boat with skill. Through his widely open white silk shirt showed his broad, muscular breast, burned brown by the sun.

The muscles of his heavy, bronzed arms rippled as he pulled the oars with an almost feline ease of motion. A fierce vitality that was evident in each feature and motion set him apart from the common men; yet his expression was neither savage nor somber, though the smoldering blue eyes hinted at ferocity easily wakened. This was Conan, who had wandered into the armed camps of the kozaks with no other possession than his wits and his sword, and who had carved his way to leadership among them.

He paddled to the carven stair as one familiar with his environs and moored the boat to a projection of the rock. Then he went up the worn steps without hesitation. He was keenly alert, not because he consciously suspected hidden danger, but because alertness was a part of him, whetted by the wild existence he followed.

What Ghaznavi had considered animal intuition or some sixth sense was merely the razor-edged faculties and savage wit of the barbarian. Conan had no instinct to tell him that men were watching him from a covert among the reeds of the mainland.

As he climbed the cliff, one of these men breathed deeply and stealthily lifted a bow. Jehungir caught his wrist and hissed an oath into his ear. "Fool! Will you betray us? Don't you realize he is out of range? Let him get upon the island. He will go looking for the girl. We will stay here awhile. He may have sensed our presence or guessed our plot. He may have warriors hidden somewhere. We will wait. In an hour, if nothing suspicious occurs, we'll row up to the foot of the stair and wait him there. If he does not return in a reasonable time, some of us will go upon the island and hunt him down. But I do not wish to do that if it can be helped. Some of us are sure to die if we have to go into the bush after him. I had rather catch him with arrows from a safe distance."

Meanwhile, the unsuspecting kozak had plunged into a forest. He went silently in his soft leather boots, his gaze sifting every shadow in eagerness to catch sight of the splendid, tawny-haired beauty of whom he had dreamed ever since he had seen her in the pavilion of Jehungir Agha by Fort

Ghori. He would have desired her even if she had displayed repugnance toward him. But her cryptic smiles and glances had fired his blood, and with all the lawless violence which was his heritage he desired that white-skinned, golden-haired woman of civilization.

He had been on Xapur before. Less than a month ago, he had held a secret conclave here with a pirate crew. He knew that he was approaching a point where he could see the mysterious ruins which gave the island its name, and he wondered if he could find the girl hiding among them. Even with the thought, he stopped as though struck dead.

Ahead of him, among the trees, rose something that his reason told him was not possible. It was a great dark green wall, with towers rearing beyond the battlements.

Conan stood paralyzed in the disruption of the faculties which demoralizes anyone who is confronted by an impossible negation of sanity. He doubted neither his sight nor his reason, but something was monstrously out of joint. Less than a month ago, only broken ruins had showed among the trees. What human hands could rear such a mammoth pile as now met his eyes, in the few weeks which had elapsed? Besides, the buccaneers who roamed Vilyet ceaselessly would have learned of any work going on on such stupendous scale and would have informed the kozaks.

There was no explaining this thing, but it was so. he was on Xapur, and that fantastic heap of towering masonry was on Xapur, and all was madness and paradox; yet it was all true.

He wheeled to race back through the jungle, down the carven stair and across the blue waters to the distant camp at the mouth of the Zaporoska. In that moment of unreasoning panic, even the thought of halting so near the inland sea was repugnant. He would leave it behind him, would quit the armed camps and the steppes and put a thousand miles between him and the blue, mysterious East where the most basic laws of nature could be set at naught, by what diabolism he could not guess.

For an instant, the future fate of kingdoms that hinged on this gay-clad barbarian hung in the balance. It was a small thing that tipped the scales — merely a shred of silk hanging on a bush that caught his uneasy glance. He leaned to it, his nostrils expanding, his nerves quivering to a subtle stimulant. On that bit of torn cloth, so faint that it was less with his physical faculties than by some obscure instinctive sense that he recognized it, lingered the tantalizing perfume that he connected with the sweet, firm flesh of the woman he had seen in Jehugir's pavilion. The fisherman had not lied, then; she was here! Then in the soil he saw a single track in the loam, the track of a bare foot, long and slender, but a man's, not a woman's, and sunk deeper than was natural. The conclusion was obvious; the man who made that track was carrying a burden, and what should it be but the girl the kozak was seeking?

He stood silently facing the dark towers that loomed through the trees, his eyes slits of blue balefire. Desire for the yellow-haired woman vied with a sullen, primordial rage at whoever had taken her. His human passion fought down his ultra-human fears, and dropping into the stalking crouch of a hunting panther, he glided toward the walls, taking advantage of the dense foliage to escape detection from the battlements.

As he approached, he saw that the walls were composed of the same green stone that had formed the ruins, and he was haunted by a vague sense of familiarity. It was as if he looked upon something he had never before seen but had dreamed of or pictured mentally. At last he recognized the sensation. The walls and towers followed the plan of the ruins. It was as if the crumbling lines had grown back into the structures they originally were.

No sound disturbed the morning quiet as Conan stole to the foot of the wall, which rose sheer from the luxuriant growth. On the southern reaches of the inland sea, the vegetation was almost tropical. He saw no one on the battlements, heard no sounds within. He saw a massive gate a short distance to his left and had no reason to suppose that it was not locked and guarded. But he believed that the woman he sought was somewhere beyond that wall, and the course he took was characteristically reckless.

Above him, vine-festooned branches reached out toward the battlements. He went up a great tree like a cat, and reaching a point above the parapet, he gripped a thick limb with both hands, swung back and forth at arm's length until he had gained momentum, and then let go and catapulted through the air, landing catlike on the battlements. Crouching there, he stared down into the streets of a city.

The circumference of the wall was not great, but the number of green stone buildings it contained was surprising. They were three or four stories in height, mainly flat-roofed, reflecting a fine architectural style. The streets converged like the spokes of a wheel into an octagon-shaped court in the centre of the town, which gave upon a lofty edifice, which, with its domes and towers, dominated the whole city. He saw no one moving in the streets or looking out of the windows, though the sun was already coming up. The silence that reigned there might have been that of a dead and deserted city. A narrow stone stair ascended the wall near him; down this he went.

Houses shouldered so closely to the wall that halfway down the stair, he found himself within arm's length of a window and halted to peer in. There were no bars, and the silk curtains were caught back with satin cords. He looked into a chamber whose walls were hidden by dark velvet tapestries. The floor was covered with thick rugs, and there were benches of polished ebony and an ivory dais heaped with furs.

He was about to continue his descent, when he heard the sound of someone approaching in the street below. Before the unknown person could round a corner and see him on the stair, he stepped quickly across the intervening space and dropped lightly into the room, drawing his scimitar. He stood for an instant statue-like; then, as nothing happened, he was moving across the rugs toward an arched doorway, when a hanging was drawn aside, revealing a cushioned alcove from which a slender, dark-haired girl regarded him with languid eyes.

Conan glared at her tensely, expecting her momentarily to start screaming. But she merely smothered a yawn with a dainty hand, rose from the alcove, and leaned negligently against the hanging which she held with one hand.

She was undoubtedly a member of a white race, though her skin was very dark. Her square-cut hair was black as midnight, her only garment a wisp of silk about her supple hips.

Presently she spoke, but the tongue was unfamiliar to him, and he shook his head. She yawned again, stretched lithely and, without any show of fear or surprise, shifted to a language he did understand, a dialect of Yuetshi which sounded strangely archaic.

"Are you looking for someone?" she asked, as indifferently as if the invasion of her chamber by an armed stranger were the most common thing imaginable.

"Who are you?" he demanded.

"I am Yateli," she answered languidly. "I must have feasted late last night, I am so sleepy now. Who are you?"

"I am Conan, a hetman among the kozaks," he answered, watching her narrowly. He believed her attitude to be a pose and expected her to try to escape from the chamber or rouse the house. But, though a velvet rope that might be a signal cord hung near her, she did not reach for it.

"Conan," she repeated drowsily. "You are not a Dagonian. I suppose you are a mercenary. Have you cut the heads off many Yuetshi?"

"I do not war on water rats!" he snorted.

"But they are very terrible," she murmured. "I remember when they were our slaves. But they revolted and burned and slew. Only the magic of Khosatral Khel has kept them from the walls—" she paused, a puzzled look struggling with the sleepiness of her expression. "I forgot," she muttered. "They did climb the walls, last night. There was shouting and fire, and the people calling in vain on Khosatral." She shook her head as if to clear it. "But that cannot be," she murmured, "because I am alive, and I thought I was dead. Oh, to the devil with it!"

She came across the chamber, and taking Conan's hand, drew him to the dais. He yielded in bewilderment and uncertainty. The girl smiled at him like a sleepy child; her long silky lashes drooped over dusky, clouded eyes. She ran her fingers through his thick black locks as if to assure herself of his reality.

"It was a dream," she yawned. "Perhaps it's all a dream. I feel like a dream now. I don't care. I can't remember something — I have forgotten — there is something I cannot understand, but I grow so sleepy when I try to think. Anyway, it doesn't matter."

"What do you mean?" he asked uneasily. "You said they climbed the walls last night? Who?"

"The Yuetshi. I thought so, anyway. A cloud of smoke hid everything, but a naked, bloodstained devil caught me by the throat and drove his knife into my breast. Oh, it hurt! But it was a dream, because see, there is no scar." She idly inspected her smooth bosom, and then sank upon Conan's lap and passed her supple arms about his massive neck. "I cannot remember," she murmured, nestling her dark head against his mighty breast. "Everything is dim and misty. It does not matter. You are no dream. You are strong. Let us live while we can. Love me!"

He cradled the girl's glossy head in the bend of his heavy arm and kissed her full red lips with unfeigned relish.

"You are strong," she repeated, her voice waning. "Love me — love —" The sleepy murmur faded away; the dusky eyes closed, the long lashes drooping over the sensuous cheeks; the supple body relaxed in Conan's arms.

He scowled down at her. She seemed to partake of the illusion that haunted this whole city, but the firm resilience of her limbs under his questing fingers convinced him that he had a living human girl in his arms, and not the shadow of a dream. No less disturbed, he hastily laid her on the furs upon the dais. Her sleep was too deep to be natural. He decided that she must be an addict of some drug, perhaps like the black lotus of Xuthal.

Then he found something else to make him wonder. Among the furs on the dais was a gorgeous spotted skin, whose predominant hue was golden. It was not a clever copy, but the skin of an actual beast. And that beast, Conan knew, had been extinct for at least a thousand years; it was the great golden leopard which figures so prominently in Hyborian legendry, and which the ancient artists delighted to portray in pigments and marble.

Shaking his head in bewilderment, Conan passed through the archway into a winding corridor. Silence hung over the house, but outside he heard a sound which his keen ears recognized as something ascending the stair on the wall from which he had entered the building. An instant later he was startled to hear something land with a soft but weighty thud on the floor of the chamber he had just quitted. Turning quickly away, he hurried along the twisting hallway until something on the floor before him brought him to a halt.

It was a human figure, which lay half in the hall and half in an opening that obviously was normally concealed by a door, which was a duplicate of the panels of the wall. It was a man, dark and lean, clad only in a silk loincloth, with a shaven head and cruel features, and he lay as if death had struck him just as he was emerging from the panel. Conan bent above him, seeking the cause of his death, and discovered him to be merely sunk in the same deep sleep as the girl in the chamber.

But why should he select such a place for his slumbers? While meditating on the matter, Conan was galvanized by a sound behind him. Something was moving up the corridor in his direction. A quick glance down it showed that it ended in a great door, which might be locked. Conan jerked the supine body out of the panel entrance and stepped through, pulling the panel shut after him. A click told him it was locked in place. Standing in utter darkness, he heard a shuffling tread halt just outside the door, and a faint chill trickled along his spine. That was no human step, nor that of any beast he had ever encountered.

There was an instant of silence, then a faint creak of wood and metal. Putting out his hand he felt the door straining and bending inward, as if a great weight were being steadily borne against it from the outside. As he reached for his sword, this ceased and he heard a strange, slobbering mouthing that prickled the short hairs on his scalp. Scimitar in hand, he began backing away, and his heels felt steps, down which he nearly tumbled. He was in a narrow staircase leading downward.

He groped his way down in the blackness, feeling for, but not finding, some other opening in the walls. Just as he decided that he was no longer in the house, but deep in the earth under it, the steps ceased in a level tunnel.

V

Along the dark, silent tunnel Conan groped, momentarily dreading a fall into some unseen pit; but at last his feet struck steps again, and he went up them until he came to a door on which his fumbling fingers found a metal catch. He came out into a dim and lofty room of enormous proportions. Fantastic columns marched about the mottled walls, upholding a ceiling, which, at once translucent and dusky, seemed like a cloudy midnight sky, giving an illusion of impossible height. If any light filtered in from the outside, it was curiously altered.

In a brooding twilight, Conan moved across the bare green floor. The great room was circular, pierced on one side by the great, bronze valves of a giant door. Opposite this, on a dais against the wall, up to which led broad curving steps, there stood a throne of copper, and when Conan saw what was coiled on this throne, he retreated hastily, lifting his scimitar.

Then, as the thing did not move, he scanned it more closely and presently mounted the glass steps and stared down at it. It was a gigantic snake, apparently carved of some jadelike substance. Each scale stood out as distinctly as in real life, and the iridescent colors were vividly reproduced. The great wedge-shaped head was half submerged in the folds of its trunk; so neither the eyes nor jaws were visible. Recognition stirred in his mind. The snake was evidently meant to represent one of those grim monsters of the marsh, which in past ages had haunted the reedy edges of Vilayet's southern shores. But, like the golden leopard, they had been extinct for hundreds of years. Conan had seen rude images of them, in minature, among the idol huts of the Yuetshi, and there was a description of them in the Book of Skelos, which drew on prehistoric sources.

Conan admired the scaly torso, thick as his thigh and obviously of great length, and he reached out and laid a curious hand on the thing. And as he did so, his heart nearly stopped. An icy chill congealed the blood in his veins and lifted the short hair on his scalp. Under his hand there was not the smooth, brittle surface of glass or metal or stone, but the yielding, fibrous mass of a living thing. He felt cold, sluggish life flowing under his fingers.

His hand jerked back in instinctive repulsion. Sword shaking in his grasp, horror and revulsion and fear almost choking him, he backed away and down the glass steps with painful care, glaring in awful fascinastion at the grisly thing that slumbered on the copper throne. It did not move.

He reached the bronze door and tried it, with his heart in his teeth, sweating with fear that he should find himself locked in with that slimy horror. But the valves yielded to his touch, and he glided though and closed them behind him.

He found himself in a wide hallway with lofty, tapestried walls, where the light was the same twilight gloom. It made distant objects indistinct, and that made him uneasy, rousing thoughts of serpents gliding unseen through the dimness. A door at the other end seemed miles away in the illusive light. Nearer at hand, the tapestry hung in such a way as to suggest an opening behind it, and lifting it cautiously he discovered a narrow stair leading up.

While he hesitated he heard, in the great room he had just left, the same shuffling tread he had heard outside the locked panel. Had he been followed through the tunnel? He went up the stair hastily, dropping the tapestry in place behind him.

Emerging presently into a twisting corridor, he took the first doorway he came to. He had a twofold purpose in his apparently aimless prowling; to escape from the building and its mysteries, and to find the Nemedian girl who, he felt, was imprisoned somewhere in this palace, temple, or whatever it was. He believed it was the great domed edifice at the center of the city, and it was likely that here dwelt the ruler of the town, to whom a captive woman would doubtless be brought.

He found himself in a chamber, not another corridor, and was about to retrace his steps, when he heard a voice which came from behind one of the walls. There was no door in that wall, but he leaned close and heard distinctly. And an icy chill crawled slowly along his spine. The tongue was Nemedian, but the voice was not human. There was a terifying resonance about it, like a bell tolling at midnight.

"There was no life in the Abyss, save that which was incorporated in me," it tolled. "Nor was there light, nor motion, nor any sound. Only the urge behind and beyond life guided and impelled me on my upward journey, blind, insensate, inexorable. Through ages upon ages, and the changeless strata of darkness I climbed—"

Ensorcelled by that belling resonance, Conan crouched forgetful of all else, until its hypnotic power caused a strange replacement of faculties and perception, and sound created the illusion of sight. Conan was no longer aware of the voice, save as far-off rhythmical waves of sound. Transported beyond his age and his own individuality, he was seeing the transmutation of the being men called Khosatral Khel which crawled up from Night and the Abyss ages ago to clothe itself in the substance of the material universe.

But human flesh was too frail, too paltry to hold the terrific essence that was Khosatral Khel. So he stood up in the shape and aspect of a man, but his flesh was not flesh; nor the bone, bone; nor blood, blood. He became a blasphemy against all nature, for he caused to live and think and act a basic substance that before had never known the pulse and stir of animate being.

He stalked through the world as a god, for no earthly weapon could harm him, and to him a century was like an hour. In his wanderings he came upon a primitive people inhabiting the island of Dagonia, and it pleased him to give this race culture and civilization, and by his aid they built the city of Dagon and they abode there and worshipped him. Strange and grisly were his servants, called from the dark corners of the planet where grim survivals of forgotten ages yet lurked. His house in Dagon was connected with every other house by tunnels through which his shaven-headed priests bore victims for the sacrifice.

But after many ages, a fierce and brutish people appeared on the shores of the sea. They called themselves Yuetshi, and after a fierce battle were defeated and enslaved, and for nearly a generation they died on the altars of Khosatral.

His sorcery kept them in bonds. Then their priest, a strange, gaunt man of unknown race, plunged into the wilderness, and when he returned he bore a knife that was of no earthly substance. It was forged of a meteor, which flashed through the sky like a flaming arrow and fell in a far valley. The slaves rose. Their saw-edged crescents cut down the men of Dagon like sheep, and against that unearthly knife the magic of Khosatral was impotent. While carnage and slaughter bellowed through the red smoke that choked the streets, the grimmest act of that grim drama was played in the cryptic dome behind the great daised chamber with its copper throne and its walls mottled like the skin of serpents.

From that dome, the Yuetshi priest emerged alone. He had not slain his foe, because he wished to hold the threat of his loosing over the heads of his own rebellious subjects. He had left Khosatral lying upon the golden dais with the mystic knife across his breast for a spell to hold him senseless and inanimate until doomsday.

But the ages passed and the priest died, the towers of deserted Dagon crumbled, the tales became dim, and the Yuetshi were reduced by plagues and famines and war to scattered remnants, dwelling in squalor along the seashore.

Only the cryptic dome resisted the rot of time, until a chance thunderbolt and the curiosity of a fisherman lifted from the breast of the god the magic knife and broke the spell. Khosatral Khel rose and lived and waxed mighty once more. It pleased him to restore the city as it was in the days before its fall. By his necromancy he lifted the towers from the dust of forgotten millenia, and the folk which had been dust for ages moved in life again.

But folk who have tasted of death are only partly alive. In the dark corners of their souls and minds, death still lurks unconquered. By night the people of Dagon moved and loved, hated and feasted, and remembered the fall of Dagon and their own slaughter only as a dim dream; they moved in an enchanted mist of illusion, feeling the strangeness of their existence but not inquiring the reasons therefor. With the coming of day, they sank into deep sleep, to be roused again only by the coming of night, which is akin to death.

All this rolled in a terrible panorama before Conan's consciousness as he crouched beside the tapestried wall. His reason stasggered. All certainty and sanity were swept away, leaving a shadowy universe through which stole hooded figures of grisly potentialities. Through the belling of the voice, which was like a tolling of triumph over the ordered laws of a sane planet, a human sound anchored Conan's mind from its flight through spheres of madness. It was the hysterical sobbing of a woman.

Involuntarily he sprung up.

VI

Jehungir Agha waited with growing impatience in his boat among the reeds. More than an hour passed, and Conan had not reappeared. Doubtless he was still searching the island for the girl he thought to be hidden there. But another surmise occurred to the Agha. Suppose the hetman had left his warriors near by, and that they should grow suspicious and come to investigate his long absence? Jehungir spoke to the oarsmen, and the long boat slid from among the reeds and glided toward the carven stairs.

Leaving half a dozen men in the boat, he took the rest, ten mighty archers of Khawarizm, in spired helmets and tiger-skin cloaks. Like hunters invading the retreat of the lion, they stole forward under the trees, arrows on strings. Silence reigned over the forest except when a great green thing that might have been a parrot swirled over their heads with a low thunder of broad wings and then sped off through the trees. With a sudden gesture, Jehungir halted his party, and they stared incredulously at the towers that showed through the verdure in the distance.

"Tarim!" muttered Jehungir. "The pirates have rebuilt the ruins! Doubtless Conan is there. We must investigate this. A fortified town this close to the mainland! — Come!"

With renewed caution, they glided through the trees. The game had altered; from pursuers and hunters they had become spies.

And as they crept through the tangled gowth, the man they sought was in peril more deadly than their filigreed arrows.

Conan realized with a crawling of his skin that beyond the wall the belling voice had ceased. He stood motionless as a statue, his gaze fixed on a curtained door through which he knew that a culminating horror would presently appear.

It was dim and misty in the chamber, and Conan's hair began to lift on his scalp as he looked. He saw a head and a pair of gigantic shoulders grow out of the twilight doom. There was no sound of footsteps, but the great dusky form grew more distinct until Conan recognized the figure of a man. He was clad in sandals, a skirt, and a broad shagreen girdle. His square-cut mane was confined by a circle of gold. Conan stared at the sweep of the monstrous shoulders, the breadth of swelling breast, the bands and ridges and clusters of muscles on torso and limbs. The face was without weakness and without mercy. The eyes were balls of dark fire. And Conan knew that this was Khosatral Khel, the ancient from the Abyss, the god of Dagonia.

No word was spoken. No word was necessary. Khosatral spread his great arms, and Conan, crouching beneath them, slashed at the giant's belly. Then he bounded back, eyes blazing with surprise. The keen edge had rung on the mighty body as on an anvil, rebounding without cutting. Then Khosatral came upon him in an irresistible surge.

There was a fleeting concussion, a fierce writhing and intertwining of limbs and bodies, and then Conan sprang clear, every thew quivering from the violence of his efforts; blood started where the grazing fingers had torn the skin. In that instant of contact, he had experienced the ultimate madness of blasphemed nature; no human flesh had bruised his, but metal animated and sentient; it was a body of living iron which opposed his.

Khosatral loomed above the warrior in the gloom. Once let those great fingers lock and they would not loosen until the human body hung limp in their grasp. In that twilit chamber it was as if a man fought with a dream-monster in a nightmare.

Flinging down his useless sword, Conan caught up a heavy bench and hurled it with all his power. It was such a missile as few men could even lift. On Khosatral's mighty breast it smashed into shreds and splinters. It did not even shake the giant on his braced legs. His face lost something of its human aspect, a nimbus of fire played about his awesome head, and like a moving tower he came on.

With a desperate wrench Conan ripped a whole section of tapestry from the wall and whirling it, with a muscular effort greater than that required for throwing the bench, he flung it over the giant's head. For an instant Khosatral floundered, smothered and blinded by the clinging stuff that resisted his strength as wood or steel could not have done, and in that instant Conan caught up his scimitar and shot out into the corridor. Without checking his speed, he hurled himself through the door of the adjoining chamber, slammed the door, and shot the bolt.

Then as he wheeled, he stopped short, all the blood in him seeming to surge to his head. Crouching on a heap of silk cushions, golden hair streaming over her naked shoulders, eyes blank with terror, was the woman for whom he had dared so much. He almost forgot the horror at his heels until a splintering crash behind him brought him to his senses. He caught up the girl and sprang for the opposite door. She was too helpless with fright either to resist or to aid him. A faint whimper was the only sound of which she seemed capable.

Conan wasted no time trying the door. A shattering stroke of his scimitar hewed the lock asunder, and as he sprang through to the stair that loomed beyond it, he saw the head and shoulders of Khosatral crash through the other door. The colossus was splintering the massive panels as if they were of cardboard.

Conan raced up the stair, carrying the big girl over one shoulder as easily as if she had been a child. Where he was going he had no idea, but the stair ended at the door of a round, domed chamber. Khosatral was coming up the stair behind them, silently as a wind of death, and as swiftly.

The chamber's walls were of solid steel, and so was the door. Conan shut it and dropped in place the great bars with which it was furnished. The thought struck him that this was Khosatral's chamber, where he locked himself in to sleep securely from the monsters he had loosed from the Pits to do his bidding.

Hardly were the bolts in place when the great door shook and trembled to the giant's assault. Conan shrugged his shoulders. This was the end of the trail. There was no other door in the chamber, nor any window. Air, and the strange misty light, evidently came from interstices in the dome. He tested the nicked edge of his scimitar, quite cool now that he was at bay. He had done his volcanic best to escape; when the giant came crashing through that door, he would explode in another savage onslaught with the useless sword, not because he expected it to do any good, but because it was his nature to die fighting. For the moment there was no course of action to take, and his calmness was not forced or feigned.

The gaze he turned on his fair companion was as admiring and intense as if he had a hundred years to live. He had dumped her unceremoniously on the floor when he turned to close the door, and she had risen to her knees, mechanically arranging her streaming locks and her scanty garment. Conan's fierce eyes glowed with approval as they devoured her thick golden hair, her clear, wide eyes, her milky skin, sleek with exuberant health, the firm swell of her breasts, the contours of her splendid hips.

A low cry escaped her as the door shook and a bolt gave way with a groan.

Conan did not look around. He knew the door would hold a little while longer.

"They told me you had escaped," he said. "A Yuetshi fisher told me you were hiding here. What is your name?"

"Octavia," she gasped mechanically. Then words came in a rush. She caught at him with desperate fingers. "Oh Mitra! what nightmare is this? The people — the dark-skinned people — one of them caught me in the forest and brought me here. They carried me to — to that — that thing. He told me — he said — am I mad? Is this a dream?"

He glanced at the door which bulged inward as if from the impact of a battering-ram.

"No," he said; "it's no dream. That hinge is giving way. Strange that a devil has to break down a door like a common man; but after all, his strength itself is a diabolism."

"Can you not kill him?" she panted. "You are strong."

Conan was too honest to lie to her. "If a mortal man could kill him, he'd be dead now," he answered. "I nicked my blade on his belly."

Her eyes dulled. "Then you must die, and I must — oh Mitra!" she screamed in sudden frenzy, and Conan caught her hands, fearing that she would harm herself. "He told me what he was going to do to me!" she panted. "Kill me! Kill me with your sword before he bursts the door!"

Conan looked at her and shook his head.

"I'll do what I can," he said. "That won't be much, but it'll give you a chance to get past him down the stair. Then run for the cliffs. I have a boat tied at the foot of the steps. If you can get out of the palace, you may escape him yet. The people of this city are all asleep."

She dropped her head in her hands. Conan took up his scimitar and moved over to stand before the echoing door. One watching him would not have realized that he was waiting for a death he regarded as inevitable. His eyes smoldered more vividly; his muscular hand knotted harder on his hilt; that was all.

The hinges had given under the giant's terrible assault, and the door rocked crazily, held only by the bolts. And these solid steel bars were buckling, bending, bulging out of their sockets. Conan watched in an almost impersonal fascination, envying the monster his inhuman strength.

Then, without warning, the bombardment ceased. In the stillness, Conan heard other noises on the landing outside — the beat of wings, and a muttering voice that was like the whining of wind through midnight branches.

Then presently there was silence, but there was a new feel in the air. Only the whetted instincts of barbarism could have sensed it, but Conan knew, without seeing or hearing him leave, that the master of Dagon no longer stood outside the door.

He glared through a crack that had been started in the steel of the portal. The landing was empty. He drew the warped bolts and cautiously pulled aside the sagging door. Khosatral was not on the stair, but far below he heard the clang of a metal door. He did not know whether the giant was plotting new deviltries or had been summoned away by that muttering voice, but he wasted no time in conjectures.

He called to Octavia, and the new note in his voice brought her up to her feet and to his side almost without her conscious volition.

"What is it?" she gasped.

"Don't stop to talk!" He caught her wrist. "Come on!" The chance for action had transformed him; his eyes blazed, his voice crackled. "The knife!" he muttered, while almost dragging the girl down the stair in his fierce haste. "The magic Yuetshi blade! He left it in the dome! I—" his voice died suddenly as a clear mental picture sprang up before him. That dome adjoined the great room where stood the copper throne — sweat started out on his body. The only way to that dome was through that room with the copper throne and the foul thing that slumbered in it.

But he did not hesitate. Swiftly they descended the stair, crossed the chamber, descended the next stair, and came into the great dim hall with its mysterious hangings. They had seen no sign of the colossus. Halting before the great bronze-valved door, Conan caught Octavia by her shoulders and shook her in his intensity.

"Listen!" he snapped. "I'm going into the room and fasten the door. Stand here and listen; if Khosatral comes, call to me. If you hear me cry out for you to go, run as though the Devil were on your heels — which he probably will be. Make for that door at the other end of the hall, because I'll be past helping you. I'm going for the Yuetshi knife!"

Before she could voice the protest her lips were framing, he had slid through the valves and shut them behind him. He lowered the bolt cautiously, not noticing that it could be worked from the outside. In the dim twilight his gaze sought that grim copper throne; yes, the scaly brute was still there, filling the throne with its loathsome coils. He saw a door behind the throne and knew that it led into the dome. But to reach it he must mount the dais, a few feet from the throne itself.

A wind blowing across the green floor would have made more noise than Conan's slinking feet. Eyes glued on the sleeping reptile he reached the dais and mounted the glass steps. The snake had not moved. He was reaching for the door . . .

The bolt on the bronze portal clanged and Conan stifled an awful oath as he saw Octavia come into the room. She stared about, uncertain in the deeper gloom, and he stood frozen, not daring to shout a warning. Then she saw his shadowy figure and ran toward the dais, crying: "I want to go with you! I'm afraid to stay alone — oh!" She threw up her hands with a terrible scream as for the first time she saw the occupant of the throne. The wedge-shaped head had lifted from its coils and thrust out toward her on a yard of shining neck.

Then with a smooth, flowing motion, it began to ooze from the throne, coil by coil, its ugly head bobbing in the direction of the paralyzed girl.

Conan cleared the space between him and the throne with a desperate bound, his scimitar swinging with all his power. And with such blinding speed did the serpent move that it whipped about and met him in full midair, lapping his limbs and body with half a dozen coils. His half-checked stroke fell futilely as he crashed down on the dais, gashing the scaly trunk but not severing it.

Then he was writhing on the glass steps with fold after slimy fold knotting about him, twisting, crushing, killing him. His right arm was still free, but he could get no purchase to strike a killing blow, and he knew one blow must suffice.

With a groaning convulsion of muscular expansion that bulged his veins almost to bursting on his temples and tied his muscles in quivering, tortured knots, he heaved up on his feet, lifting almost the full weight of that forty-foot devil.

An instant he reeled on wide-braced legs, feeling his ribs caving in on his vitals and his sight growing dark, while his scimitar gleamed above his head. Then it fell, shearing through the scales and flesh and vertebrae. And where there had been one huge, writhing cable, now there were horribly two, lashing and flopping in the death throes. Conan staggered away from their blind strokes. He was sick and dizzy, and blood oozed from his nose. Groping in a dark mist he clutched Octavia and shook her until she gasped for breath.

"Next time I tell you to stay somewhere," he gasped, "you stay!"

He was too dizzy even to know whether she replied. Taking her wrist like a truant schoolgirl, he led her around the hideous stumps that still loomed and knotted on the floor. Somewhere, in the distance, he thought he heard men yelling, but his ears were still roaring so that he could not be sure.

The door gave to his efforts. If Khosatral had placed the snake there to guard the thing he feared, evidently he considered it ample precaution. Conan half expected some other monstrosity to leap at him with the opening of the door, but in the dimmer light he saw only the vague sweep of the arch above, a dully gleaming block of gold, and a half-moon glimmer on the stone.

With a gasp of gratification, he scooped it up and did not linger for further exploration. He turned and fled across the room and down the great hall toward the distant door that he felt led to the outer air. He was correct. A few minutes later he emerged into the silent streets, half carrying, half guiding his companion. There was no one to be seen, but beyond the western wall there sounded cries and moaning wails that made Octavia tremble. He led her to the southwestern wall and without difficulty found a stone stair that mounted the rampart. He had appropriated a thick tapestry rope in the great hall, and now, having reached the parapet, he looped the soft, strong cord about the girl's hips and lowered her to the earth. Then, making one end fast to a merlon, he slid down after her. There was but one way of escape from the island — the stair on the western cliffs. In that direction he hurried, swinging wide around the spot from which had come the cries and the sound of terrible blows.

Octavia sensed that grim peril lurked in those leafy fastnesses. Her breath came pantingly and she pressed close to her protector. But the forest was silent now, and they saw no shape of menace until they emerged from the trees and glimpsed a figure standing on the edge of the cliffs.

Jehungir Agha had escaped the doom that had overtaken his warriors when an iron giant sallied suddenly from the gate and battered and crushed them into bits of shredded flesh and splintered bone. When he saw the swords of his archers break on that manlike juggernaut, he had known it was no human foe they faced, and he had fled, hiding in the deep woods until the sounds of slaughter ceased. Then he crept back to the stair, but his boatmen were not waiting for him.

They had heard the screams, and presently, waiting nervously, had seen, on the cliff above them, a blood-smeared monster waving gigantic arms in awful triumph. They had waited for no more. When Jehungir came upon the cliffs, they were just vanishing among the reeds beyond earshot. Khosatral was gone — had either returned to the city or was prowling the forest in search of the man who had escaped him outside the walls.

Jehungir was just preparing to descend the stairs and depart in Conan's boat, when he saw the hetman and the girl emerge from the trees. The experience which had congealed his blood and almost blasted his reason had not altered Jehungir's intentions towards the kozak chief. The sight of the man he had come to kill filled him with gratification. He was astonished to see the girl he had given to Jelal Khan, but he wasted no time on her. Lifting his bow he drew the shaft to its head and loosed. Conan crouched and the arror splintered on a tree, and Conan laughed.

"Dog!" he taunted. "You can't hit me! I was not born to die on Hyrkanian steel! Try again, pig of Turan!"

Jehungir did not try again. That was his last arrow. He drew his scimitar and advanced, confident in his spired helmet and close-meshed mail. Conan met him halfway in a blinding whirl of swords. The curved blades ground together, sprang apart, circled in glittering arcs that blurred the sight which tried to follow them. Octavia, watching, did not see the stroke, but she heard its chopping impact and saw Jehungir fall, blood spurting from his side where the Cimmerian's steel had sundered his mail and bitten to his spine.

But Octavia's scream was not caused by the death of her former master. With a crash of bending boughs, Khosatral Khel was upon them. The girl could not flee; a moaning cry escaped her as her knees gave way and pitched her groveling to the sward.

Conan, stooping above the body of the Agha, made no move to escape. Shifting his reddened scimitar to his left hand, he drew the great half-blade of the Yuetshi. Khosatral Khel was towering above him, his arms lifted like mauls, but as the blade caught the sheen of the sun, the giant gave back suddenly.

But Conan's blood was up. He rushed in, slashing with the crescent blade. And it did not splinter. Under its edge, the dusky metal of Khosatral's body gave way like common flesh beneath a cleaver. From the deep gash flowed a strange ichor, and Khosatral cried out like the dirging of a great bell. His terrible arms flailed down, but Conan, quicker than the archers who had died beneath those awful flails, avoided their strokes and struck again and yet again. Khosatral reeled and tottered; his cries were awful to hear, as if metal were given a tongue of pain, as if iron shrieked and bellowed under torment.

Then, wheeling away, he staggered into the forest; he reeled in his gait, crashed through bushes, and caromed off trees. Yet though Conan followed him with the speed of hot passion, the walls and towers of Dagon loomed through the trees before the man came with dagger-reach of the giant.

Then Khosatral turned again, flailing the air with desperate blows, but Conan, fired to beserk fury, was not to be denied. As a panther strikes down a bull moose at bay, so he plunged under the bludgeoning arms and drove the crescent blade to the hilt under the spot wheer a human's heart would be.

Khosatral reeled and fell. In the shape of a man he reeled, but it was not the shape of a man that struck the loam. Where there had been the likeness of a human face, there was no face at all, and the metal limbs melted and changed

. . . Conan, who had not shrunk from Khosatral living, recoiled blenching for Khosatral dead, for he had witnessed an awful transmutation; in his dying throes Khosatral Khel had become again the thing that had crawled up from the Abyss millennia gone. Gagging with intolerable repugnance, Conan turned to flee the sight; and he was suddenly aware that the pinnacles of Dagon no longer glimmered through the trees. They had faded like smoke — the battlements, the crenellated towers, the great bronze gates, the velvets, the gold, the ivory, and the dark-haired women, and the men with their shaven skulls. With the passing of the inhuman intellect which had given them rebirth, they had faded back into the dust which they had been for ages uncounted. Only the stumps of broken columns rose above crumbling walls and broken paves and shattered dome. Conan again looked upon the ruins of Xapur as he remembered them.

The wild hetman stood like a statue for a space, dimly grasping something of the cosmic tragedy of the fitful ephemera called mankind and the hooded shapes of darkness which prey upon it. Then as he heard his voice called in accents of fear, he started, as one awakening from a dream, glanced again at the thing on the ground, shuddered and turned away toward the cliffs and the girl that waited there.

She was peering fearfully under the trees, and she greeted him with a half-stifled cry of relief. He had shaken off the dim monstrous visions which had momentarily haunted him, and was his exuberant self again.

"Where is he?" she shuddered.

"Gone back to Hell whence he crawled," he replied cheerfully. "Why didn't you climb the stair and make your escape in my boat?"

"I wouldn't desert—" she began, then changed her mind, and amended rather sulkily, "I have nowhere to go. The Hyrkanians would enslave me again, and the pirates would—"

"What of the kozaks?" he suggested.

"Are they better than the pirates?" she asked scornfully. Conan's admiration increased to see how well she had recovered her poise after having endured such frantic terror. Her arrogance amused him.

"You seemed to think so in the camp by Ghori," he answered. "You were free enough with your smiles then."

Her red lips curled in disdain. "Do you think I was enamored of you? Do you dream that I would have shamed myself before an ale-guzzling, meat-gorging barbarian unless I had to? My master — whose body lies there — forced me to do as i did."

"Oh!" Conan seemed rather crestfallen. Then he laughed with undiminished zest. "No matter. You belong to me now. Give me a kiss."

"You dare ask—" she began angrily, when she felt herself snatched off her feet and crushed to the hetman's muscular breast. She fought him fiercely, with all the supple strength of her magnificent youth, but he only laughed exuberantly, drunk with the possession of this splendid creature writhing in his arms.

He crushed her struggles easily, drinking the nectar of her lips with all the unrestrained passion that was his, until the arms that strained against them melted and twined convulsively about his massive neck. Then he laughed down into the clear eyes, and said: "Why should not a chief of the Free People be preferable to a city-bred dog of Turan?"

She shook back her tawny locks, still tingling in every nerve from the fire of his kisses. She did not loosen her arms from his neck. "Do you deem yourself an Agha's equal?" she challenged.

He laughed and strode with her in his arms toward the stair. "You shall judge," he boasted. "I'll burn Khawarizm for a torch to light your way to my tent."

www.ingramcontent.com/pod-product-compliance
Lightning Source LLC
Chambersburg PA
CBHW030239180626
46810CB00008B/3211